CATCH FLIES!

Tristan Howard

A
LITTLE **APPLE**
PAPERBACK

SCHOLASTIC INC.
New York   Toronto   London   Auckland   Sydney

ISBN 0-590-56924-4

Copyright © 1996 by Daniel Weiss Associates, Inc. Conceived by Ed Monagle, Michael Pollack, and Daniel Weiss. Grateful acknowledgment to Stephen Currie. All rights reserved. Published by Scholastic Inc. LITTLE APPLE PAPERBACKS and the LITTLE APPLE logo are registered trademarks of Scholastic Inc. Cover art copyright © 1996 by Daniel Weiss Associates, Inc. Interior illustrations by Marcy Ramsey.

Produced by Daniel Weiss Associates, Inc.
33 West 17th Street, New York, NY 10011

12 11 10 9 8 7 6 5 4 3 2   6 7 8 9/9 0 1/0

Printed in the U.S.A.   40

First Scholastic printing, June 1996

Chapter
1

"'Take me out to the ball game!'" Matt Carter was singing at the top of his lungs.

"'Take me out with the crowd!'" Matt's best friend, Lucy Marcus, joined in. I groaned and clapped my hands over my ears.

"Matt! Lucy!" That was my mother. I took my hands off my ears. "Pay attention!" Mom shouted.

"Yeah, pay attention," I told them.

Matt stuck out his tongue at me, and Lucy giggled. Matt, Lucy, and I all play on a baseball team called the Rangers. My mom is the coach, even though she doesn't know a thing about baseball.

1

Sometimes I think we're a great team. Other times, I wonder. Mitchell Rubin falls asleep when the other team is at bat. Alex Slavik's feet are way too big for him. And Lucy and Matt like to sing. On the bench. During a game!

"Catherine!" my mom was yelling now. "Catherine Antler!"

Oops, I thought suddenly, that's me! "What?" I asked.

"It's your turn to bat!"

Lucy and Matt burst out laughing. "Pay attention!" they told me at exactly the same time. Then Matt pointed at Lucy and said, "Jinx!"

I went up to home plate. Baseball is pretty simple. You try to hit the ball. If someone catches it in the air, you're out. You're also out if someone tags you with the ball, or if the person holding the ball steps on first base before you get there. But if you're lucky, you can go around the bases and touch home plate. Then you score a run.

I could see Alex on second base. If I hit the ball hard, he would score.

"Go, Catherine!" Mom shouted.

"Go, Catherine!" I could hear Matt and

Lucy yell together. This time it was Lucy who said it: "Jinx!"

I swung. The ball flew into the outfield. "Run, Alex!" I yelled. Then I put my head down and ran as hard as I could to first base.

"Run, Alex!" Lucy and Matt shouted. As I got to first base I could hear them laughing. "Jinx!" they said at the same time.

Alex rounded third base and kept running. He was almost to home plate when, all at once, his feet slipped out from under him. I saw him come down with a thump. But luckily he fell down right on home plate!

Let's Go Rangers!!

"Safe!" yelled the umpire.

"Rangers rule!" I shouted. That gave us fourteen runs. Fourteen for us, and only ten for the Cubs!

We might have scored again. But when it was Matt's turn to bat, he was so busy singing that he struck out.

I like Matt a lot. But sometimes I wish he would learn to pay attention.

"Go, Rangers!" I shouted as I ran to

shortstop. That's where I play. You don't have to be short to play shortstop. And it isn't a place to stop, either. It's between second and third base.

"Go, Rangers!" Lucy shouted.

"Go, Rangers!" Matt shouted. Matt was our catcher. He waved his arms in the air like a music conductor. "One, two, three—"

Everybody screamed it. "Go, Rangers!"

"Jinx!" Matt said. He pointed to Lucy and grinned. "Got you!" Lucy frowned and stuck out her lip.

The Cubs were coming up for the last time. Their first batter hit the ball to Julie Zimmer. Julie reached up—and missed the ball. The Cubs player had a double.

"Oh, dear," Mom sighed. "Hold 'em, Rangers!"

"Hold 'em, Rangers," everybody yelled. Except Lucy.

The next batter hit a ground ball to Yin Wong. Yin threw it to Lucy at first base. But Lucy couldn't quite catch it. The batter was safe.

Now the Cubs had two runners on base. And the next batter had already hit two home runs! Uh-oh, I thought. "Go back, Alex!" I called, turning to the outfield. "Eight giant steps!"

Alex took only six steps backward. Just as the batter swung, Alex tripped over his enormous feet and fell. *Wham!* The ball sailed way over Alex's head. Julie ran after it. So did Alex. After he got back up, that is.

But it didn't make any difference. It was another home run.

We got better after that. Adam Fingerhut caught a ball. So did Brenda Bailey. When the last Cub of the game came up, there was a runner on base. But we were still leading by a run, 14–13.

"Come on, Rangers!" Josh Ramos shouted. Lucy did a cartwheel.

Closing his eyes, the batter swung and missed. Then he did it again. One more strike to go!

" ' 'Cause it's one, two, three strikes you're out,' " Matt sang loudly. This time even Lucy joined in. " 'At the old ball game!' "

Matt pointed at Lucy again. "Jinx!" he yelled before she could say anything.

"Watch the game, Matt," Mom said.

The batter swung again. This time he hit the ball. It soared high in the air right near home plate. Yay! I thought. If Matt catches it, we win!

"Catch it, Matt!" Lucy told him. She ran to stand near him.

I've got it!

"I've got it!" Matt yelled. He cupped his hands—and dropped the ball.

Matt's face turned as red as a tomato. Quickly he picked up the ball and threw it to first base. But Lucy wasn't there. I watched the ball fly into right field, straight at—

Mitchell.

Who was lying there fast asleep.

"Mitchell! Wake up!" I yelled. Julie and Adam ran toward right field. "*Wake up!*" they screamed as loudly as they could.

Mitchell yawned and sat up. "What's for breakfast?" he asked, rubbing his eyes.

The runner scored. So did the batter. The Cubs cheered and jumped up and down. They had scored fifteen runs—and they were the winners.

Lucy stepped toward Matt. "Matt!" she wailed. "I wish you'd caught that ball. Now we've lost!"

Matt looked as if he was about to cry. I felt sorry for him. "Well, you should have caught my throw." He wiped his eyes on his sleeve. "But there was this really neat bug in the air, and—"

"And I wish you'd quit jinxing me!" Lucy interrupted.

"Lucy's right." Josh sounded angry. "All you had to do was catch the ball. Then we would have won."

"That's not fair," Danny West told him. "Even major league players drop the ball sometimes." Danny knows a ton about baseball.

I patted Matt's shoulder. I drop the ball sometimes, too, and I don't like it when people yell at me. "I think you're being mean, Lucy," I said.

"Yeah, Lucy," Matt said. "I thought we were friends."

"Kids, kids!" Mom put one arm around Lucy and the other arm around Matt. "It's okay. You played well. You just had some bad luck at the end." She smiled. "I'm going to treat you to ice cream anyway. Come on. Let's all yell, 'Go, Rangers!'"

"Go, Rangers," we repeated. But we didn't say it as if we meant it.

Mom raised her eyebrows. "Do I have to eat the ice cream by myself?"

"I'll help," Brenda said. "And if you guys don't want any, I'll eat yours, too."

Even though I still felt bad about losing, I didn't like Brenda's idea very much. "I'll come," I said.

"So will I," Adam said. "I guess."

Mom grinned. "But first we have to yell, 'Go, Rangers!' Ready?"

We all looked at one another. Except Matt and Lucy. They looked at the ground.

"All of us, Matt," Mom said sternly. "All of us, Lucy."

Matt looked up and caught Lucy's eye. He swallowed hard and began to grin.

"Go, Rangers!" he shouted just as Lucy shouted it, too. They pointed at each other and began to giggle.

"Jinx!" they yelled.

Chapter
2

We played the Cubs on Friday. On Monday we had practice after school. When Mom and I got to the field, Lucy and Matt were already there—playing leapfrog. Josh, his dog, and his parents were there, too.

"Hi, Catherine!" Lucy shouted. "Watch what we're doing!" She put her hands on Matt's back and hopped over. Now she was standing in front of him.

"No fair!" Matt yelled. "You stepped on my hand! It hurts!" He laughed to show he didn't really mean it.

"Sorry!" Lucy giggled. She bent down so Matt could hop over her.

9

It sure looked like fun! I was about to ask Mom if I could play, too. But suddenly Matt pushed down on Lucy's back just a little too hard. Lucy fell over with a crash. "Ow!" she screamed.

"Oops," Matt said. He stood above her with a worried look on his face.

"Are you all right?" Mom hurried over to Lucy.

"Matt knocked me down!" Lucy said as Mom helped her to her feet. "Matt! That really hurt!"

Matt bit his lip. "Well, I didn't do it on purpose," he said in a small voice.

Lucy brushed some dirt off her pants. "I bet you did," she sniffed.

"I don't think you have any cuts," Mom said to Lucy. She looked at her carefully. "I'm sure Matt didn't mean to do it. Are you all right? That's the main thing."

Lucy frowned and wiggled her fingers. "I guess."

"Okay!" Mom clapped. "Everybody over to the field! Let's play circle catch."

Lucy turned to Matt and grinned. "Race you!" she shouted, and they chased each other to home plate, laughing as they ran.

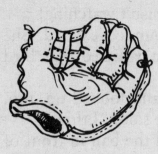

In circle catch, we toss the ball all the way around a circle, so everybody has a chance to catch it. Mom times us. So far our record is one minute thirteen seconds. That's with no one dropping the ball.

"I don't want to stand next to Josh," Julie said.

Mom frowned. "Why not, Julie?"

"Because his shirt doesn't match my shirt," Julie answered.

"They're both blue," Josh said.

"They're both blue, but they aren't the same blue," Julie told him. Julie takes clothes very seriously.

"Okay, Julie," Mom said. "Switch places with Matt."

Mitchell yawned. "I'm tired, Mrs. Antler."

Mom pretended that Mitchell hadn't said anything. She gave me a ball. "Go!"

I tossed the ball to Yin. Yin turned and tossed it to Julie. Julie caught it and passed the ball to Danny. We were going great. But

11

when Danny started to throw the ball to Lucy, he stopped. Lucy wasn't watching!

"Hey, Matt!" Lucy sounded excited. She pointed to the sky. "Can you see that bird up there?"

Matt shaded his eyes and looked up, too. "It's a Canada goose," he said. "I think."

"Lucy!" Danny waved the ball in front of her face.

"We want to beat our record!" Adam shouted.

"I don't think it's a Canada goose," Lucy told Matt. "I think it's a crow. See, the wings are black."

Matt took a couple of steps forward. "Maybe I can see better from here," he said.

"Lucy!" Danny raised his voice. But Lucy still didn't turn around.

"You're right," said Matt. "It *is* a crow. I think."

"Time out!" said Mom. "Lucy, watch what's going on, please." She took the ball back from Danny while Lucy did a cart-wheel. I shook my head. How can you watch birds in the middle of playing circle catch?

"Let's try again," Mom said. She handed the ball to me. "Ready? Go!"

We played circle catch for about ten minutes, but we couldn't beat our old record. Something always happened!

One time, Matt was drawing in the dirt with a stick. Josh threw him the ball, but Matt never even saw it. Another time, Brenda took a candy bar out of her pocket just when the ball came to her. The ball landed on the ground. And the candy bar got smushed, too.

Once we got almost all the way around the circle. Mitchell was about to catch the ball and throw it to me. But Josh's big dog came running up. I guess he thought we were playing catch with him. He grabbed the ball in his mouth and ran away. We finally got our ball back. But it was kind of wet for a while after that!

"This is no fun," Adam said at last. He sat down on the grass. "I don't want to play anymore if we keep messing up."

"One more time," Mom told him. She handed me the ball. "Go!"

I threw it to Yin. Yin threw it to Julie.

Julie grinned and tossed it to Danny. "Yay!" I said. So far we were doing really well! I watched as Danny threw it to Lucy, and Lucy threw it to Matt—

"Oh, no!" I groaned. The ball bounced next to Matt and rolled away.

"I couldn't catch that one," Matt complained. "You threw it too far from me."

"No, I didn't!" Lucy stamped her foot.

"Yes, you did!" Matt picked up the ball and stamped his foot, too. Lucy began to giggle.

"Matt, you should have caught that," Josh complained. "It's like when you dropped the ball on Friday. Now we'll *never* break our record."

"Lucy just messed up her throw," Adam told her. "If Lucy had—"

"Snack break," Mom said quickly. She handed me a bag of orange slices. Then she gave another bag to Yin. "Make sure to share them," she said.

Josh put one arm around Lucy and the other arm around Yin. "Come on," he said. "Let's go eat at the big tree. Where nobody can drop *our* orange slices."

"Come on, Matt," I said, and I put my arm around his shoulder. "We'll stay right here and eat *our* oranges. Okay?"

"Okay," Matt said happily.

"They're so mean," Adam said. He took three slices out of our bag. "Don't you think they're mean, Catherine?"

I looked over toward the tree. Yin, Lucy, Alex, Julie, and Josh were sitting there together. I thought maybe I could see Lucy and Julie pointing at us in a mean way. "Uh-huh," I said. "Just because Matt dropped one pop-up."

"And then Lucy threw the ball so hard he couldn't catch it," Adam added.

Matt stuck out his tongue at the other kids. "I guess they're just underwear heads, that's all," he said.

"Even Lucy?" Mitchell looked surprised.

Matt thought for a moment. "Even Lucy," he said at last. "But I still like her anyway." He picked up an orange slice and sucked the juice out of it. Then he stuck the whole peel into his mouth and began to make funny noises. *"Mmm, mmm, mmm!"*

"You're silly," Brenda said. She picked up the last four slices.

17

"*Mmm, mmm, mmm!*" Matt said, pointing to the peel in his mouth. I laughed. He looked as if he didn't have any teeth—just a big orange tongue.

Matt took the peel out of his mouth. "Hey, Lucy!" he shouted. When she turned to look, he stuck the peel back in and made those noises again: "*Mmm, mmm, mmm!*"

Lucy began to grin. She reached into the bag of oranges and popped a slice into her mouth, just like Matt. "*Mmm, mmm, mmm,*" she said loudly.

I had to laugh. One moment Matt calls Lucy an underwear head. Then, just like that, they're friends again!

Our game on Tuesday was against the
Orioles. I like playing the Orioles. My best
friend, Amy Powell, is on their team. So is
Michael Grassi, my other best friend.

The bad part is that Too Tall Henry plays
on the Orioles, too.

Too Tall's the biggest kid in third grade. I
barely come up to his chin. And I'm no shrimp.

Too Tall also has the biggest mouth in the
whole school. He likes to call people mean
names. Sometimes he calls me "Catherine
Antelope." He calls Julie Zimmer "Julie
Dimwit." And I won't even tell you his
names for some of the other kids.

19

The first Oriole up was Amy. She got a single. Part of me was sorry, but part of me was glad. I really like Amy. Even if she is an Oriole.

"Let's go, Rangers!" Mom shouted from the bench.

"No batter, no batter," Danny West called as the next hitter came to the plate.

NO BATTER . . . NO BATTER

Lucy yelled, "Come on, Rangers!" Then she took off her mitt and did a cartwheel.

"Lucy!" Mom shouted. "Pay attention!"

But the batter had already swung. He hit the ball right to Lucy. It would have been an easy out—except that Lucy didn't have her mitt on! She dropped the ball, and the runner was safe.

I could hardly believe my eyes. Of all the stupid times to do a cartwheel!

"Lucy!" Matt groaned. "You're supposed to catch the ball."

"You're going to make us lose!" Adam yelled from the outfield.

"Butterfingers!" Too Tall shouted.

"Keep your eye on the ball, dear," Mom suggested.

Lucy glared at Matt. "Well, I tried!" she said. "It's not like you're so great yourself, Matt Carter!"

"I never said I was great," Matt yelled back.

Lucy pulled down the corners of her eyes and stuck her tongue out of one side of her mouth. "This is you, Matt!" she said, laughing hard.

"Oh, cut it out," Matt told her. But he was beginning to laugh, too. "This is you!" He stuck out his lip and wiggled his head around.

Lucy grinned. "Well, this is you." She waved her arm in front of her nose like an elephant's trunk.

Suddenly the Orioles began to cheer.

"Catherine!" Mom yelled. I spun around. Amy was heading for third base! Something hit me in the back and bounced into the outfield.

The ball!

"Oh, no!" I said as it rolled away.

"Hey, Antelope!" Too Tall's voice was loud. "You catch the ball with your mitt—not your back!"

"Keep your eye on the ball, Catherine," Mom said.

"Catherine!" Julie rolled her eyes, and I could hear Josh yelling at me, too.

At first I was embarrassed. But then I felt angry. If Lucy hadn't been making faces at Matt, I thought, I would have been watching the batter. I could have caught the ball.

Yup, I thought. Lucy made me mess up, all right.

The Orioles scored six runs. At last it was our turn to bat. When I got to the bench, I sat down next to Matt. Lucy sat down with Julie and Josh at the other end of the bench. They started to laugh.

I looked over at them. Were they laughing at me?

I hoped not, but I couldn't tell for sure.

"Come on," Mom said as Mitchell went up to bat. "Let's hear some cheering! Go, team! Go, Rangers!"

"Go, Mitchell!" I yelled.

"Go, Mitchell!" Matt yelled at the same time. So did Danny and Adam and Brenda.

"Jinx!" I said before anyone else could.

"Jinx is such a dumb game," Julie said. "Don't you think so, Lucy?"

Lucy looked at Matt and me. Then she looked at Josh and Julie. "Um—yeah," she said at last. "I don't like being jinxed all the time."

"Jinx is *not* a dumb game," said Matt. He frowned at Lucy. "You just say that because you're not very good at it."

"I am too good at it!" Lucy said. "I'm a lot better than you are."

Matt laughed. "No, you're not," he said.

But Lucy had guessed what he was going to say. "No, you're not!" she said at exactly the same time. Then she added, "Jinx!"

"No fair," said Matt. "I said it a little before you did."

"He's right," Adam jumped in. "He did."

"No, you didn't." Lucy folded her arms. "And I think you're mean. You made fun of me on the field, and now you're trying to cheat me. I don't think that's fair."

"Yay, Mitchell!" Mom shouted. We all looked up in surprise. While we had been talking, Mitchell had gotten a double!

"Who's next?" Mom asked. "It's you, Josh."

23

"Yay, Josh!" Lucy stood up and cheered. So did Yin, Alex, and Julie. But I pretended to look at my fingernails, and Matt yawned.

"Oh, great," Adam said. "Now we'll lose for sure."

Mom sighed. "Go, Josh," she hissed at us.

"Go, Josh," I said very, very softly. Matt and I grinned. "Not!" we said together.

We both pointed. "Jinx!" At the other end of the bench, I could see Lucy roll her eyes.

"Lucy can be really annoying," I told Matt.

Matt shrugged. "Sometimes we get mad at each other," he said. "But mostly we get over it."

When Matt came up in the last inning, we were just one run behind. "Go, Matt!" I screamed.

Matt hit a single. I clapped my hands. "Don't you wish you could hit like that, Lucy?" I asked her.

"That was a bad hit," Lucy said. She had a goofy grin on her face. "He should have made it to second base."

"Third base," Josh corrected her.

"Home run!" shouted Yin.

"He didn't make it because he's so fat,"

Lucy went on. "That's why everybody calls him Fat Carter!"

I gasped. "Fat Carter" was Too Tall Henry's nickname for Matt! "Stop it, Lucy," I said. "That's mean!"

"Well, it's true," Josh said loudly. "And he always drops the ball, too."

"I do not!" Matt yelled from first base.

I clenched my fists. "You can't talk about Matt that way, Lucy Marcus! I mean—" I thought hard. "Lucy Barf-on-us!"

"Catherine!" Mom sounded shocked.

Julie hit a double, and Matt ran to third base. The kids on Lucy's end of the bench yelled, "Yay, Julie!" and the kids on Matt's end yelled, "Yay, Matt!" We could tie the game if Lucy got a hit.

Part of me wanted Lucy to get a hit—maybe even hit a home run and win the game. But another part of me wanted her to strike out.

I held my breath as Lucy swung.

She hit a hard line drive right over third base. I watched as Matt leaped up into the air and made a spectacular catch.

"Out!" screamed the umpire.

"Yes!" I shouted.

26

Matt landed on the ground and tagged Julie as she came running over to third.

"Double play!" the umpire yelled. "Game's over!"

DOUBLE PLAY

"Who said I can't catch?" Matt cried. He held up the ball for everyone to see. "What a player, huh?"

Mitchell and Adam slapped each other five. Brenda cheered. But Danny looked confused. And Lucy was shaking her head.

"You dummy!" she shouted. "You were supposed to be running!"

Matt's jaw dropped open, and he just stared at her.

Supposed to be running? I thought. All of a sudden I realized Lucy was right. Matt was the runner, not the fielder. He wasn't even wearing a mitt!

I couldn't believe it. Matt had just made his best catch ever. And he'd made it for the wrong team!

Chapter 4

"Go get the ball, Josh," I said. It was Wednesday. We were practicing before the game against the Reds.

"No way," Josh told me. "You threw it. You get it."

"You were supposed to catch it!" I yelled.

"I couldn't," Josh answered. "It was, like, six miles over my head."

"It was not!" I stamped my foot. "It was three inches."

"Okay, you two." Mom came over to us. "Josh, why don't you go practice with Alex and Matt—"

"Uhh-uh!" Josh burst out. "Matt's even

28

worse than Catherine! He's the worst on the whole team!" He folded his arms. "I'm not getting the ball, and I'm not playing with Matt."

Mitchell came running up. He dropped his practice ball and tugged on Mom's sleeve. "Mrs. Antler?"

Mom sighed. "What is it, sweetie?"

"Julie's bugging me," Mitchell told her. "She keeps looking at me."

"No, I'm not!" Julie said, coming up. "Who'd want to look at him, anyway?" She made a face. "Look at his dumb sweatshirt."

"It's a nice sweatshirt," I told Julie. Somebody had to protect Mitchell. "You're just jealous because Mitchell's a better player than you."

"He is not," Julie said. "I want to trade partners. Can't I be with Lucy? Our shoes match."

"Mrs. Antler?" Alex was standing in front of Mom. He looked worried. "I can't practice with Matt. He and Lucy keep pretending to be airplanes."

"That's because airplanes can't catch," Josh said. "Just like Matt."

I looked at Matt. His arms were stretched out like wings, and he was running around Lucy, making jet noises. "Fire one!" Lucy shouted. They were laughing loudly. I shook my head and remembered what Matt had said: "Sometimes we get mad at each other. But mostly we get over it."

Sometimes they got over it really fast!

"Matt was shooting me, too," Alex said sadly.

"You don't think those are real bullets, do you?" I demanded. For a smart person, Alex can be pretty dumb sometimes.

"He'd miss, anyway," Julie said.

"Fire two!" Matt made shooting noises.

"Hey, Matt!" I yelled. I picked up Mitchell's ball and threw it up high. I would show everybody that Matt could too catch the ball when he was supposed to. "Catch!"

Matt grinned and came running toward me, his arms stretched wide.

"Look out!" Mom cried. "Lucy!"

Lucy was turning a somersault—right in Matt's way! "Matt!" I yelled as loudly as I could. "Look out!"

There was a crash—and Lucy and Matt were lying on the ground. "You should watch where you're going!" Lucy said. Her eyes filled with tears.

"No way!" Matt said. "You should watch where *you're* going. I'll bet you rolled there on purpose. Just to bug me." He stood up slowly. So did Lucy.

"It was Matt's fault," Josh said.

"No, it was Lucy's fault," Adam argued.

"Stop!" Mom sounded mad. "You're supposed to be a team," she said firmly, "but you're not acting like one. Put down your mitts. We're going to play a game."

"What kind of game, Mrs. Antler?" Danny asked curiously.

"A teamwork game," Mom said. "Stand in a circle."

"I won't stand next to Adam," Josh said. He turned his back. "Adam stinks."

"I do not!" Adam said.

Mom ignored them. "When I say 'go,'" she told us, "you reach into the circle and grab somebody's hand. It doesn't matter whose."

Yes, it does, I thought.

"Then your hands will be all mixed up," Mom explained. "You have to untangle yourselves without letting go."

"I'm not touching Josh," Adam said loudly.

Mom took a deep breath. "Ready? Go!"

We all stuck out our hands. I reached for Matt, but he was too far away. Instead I grabbed someone else. Ugh, Julie, I thought. I let go and grabbed again.

"Danny's hand is all sweaty," Josh complained.

"That's not my hand!" Danny glared at him. "That's Alex's."

"Oh." Josh looked down. "I guess it's not that sweaty."

I tried to figure out whose hands I had. Brenda's and Mitchell's. That was okay. At least I hadn't grabbed Lucy's.

"Ready to start untangling?" Mom asked. But she was interrupted.

"Hey, Matt! Let's do London Bridge!" It was Lucy's voice.

I turned to look—and I could hardly believe my eyes.

Lucy and Matt were standing across the circle from each other, holding hands. "London Bridge is falling down!" Lucy started to sing. Matt joined in, grinning at

Lucy and swinging his arms back and forth.

"Falling down, falling down!" they sang.

I looked at Julie. She looked back at me. Together we shook our heads. Were Matt and Lucy goofy, or what?

Chapter
5

The game against the Reds didn't go very well.

The first batter hit a ground ball right to me. I was about to throw the ball to Lucy at first base. Then I decided that Lucy would probably drop it. So I ran to first and tried to beat the runner. But the batter got there first.

I think I might have tripped a little bit.

"Throw the ball next time," Mom shouted.

"But Mom—" I began. Then I saw that Mom wasn't paying attention. Sometimes she's just not a very good listener.

In the second inning, one of the Reds hit the ball to the outfield. It rolled between Adam and Josh.

"I'll throw it in," Josh told Adam. He reached down for the ball.

"No, I will." Adam grabbed Josh's arm. "You'll just mess it up."

"No, I won't! Let go!" Josh yelled. By the time they stopped fighting, the batter had a home run.

SAFE

"Teamwork!" Mom yelled from the bench.

"Yeah, teamwork!" I told Josh. "Next time let Adam get it."

By the third inning, we were already losing, 12–3. When it was our turn to bat, Lucy and Matt found sticks and started writing in the dirt next to the bench.

"Just wait till you see what I'm writing," Lucy said. She laughed.

"Oh yeah?" said Matt. "Well, just wait till you see what *I'm* writing." He turned his back so Lucy couldn't see. I looked very closely. "L-U-C-Y," I spelled out loud. "Lucy. 'Lucy is—'"

But that was all he had written so far.

"Ta-da!" Lucy jumped up. With her stick she pointed to what she had written.

"'Matt is silly,'" Matt read. A goofy grin spread over his face. "I'm not the silly one— you are!"

"No, you are!" Lucy answered. "What did you write?"

Matt dropped his stick to the ground. "I'm not telling."

"Oh, come on," Lucy begged. "Please?"

Matt grinned again and shook his head. "It's a secret."

"Matt!" Mom was calling him.

Matt looked up. "Yes, Mrs. Antler?"

"It's your turn to bat, dear," Mom told him.

Matt stood up slowly. "But Mrs. Antler, I don't want to. I'd rather stay here with Lucy and write with my stick."

I just rolled my eyes.

The Reds had scored twenty-six runs by the time the last inning began. Their first batter swung and hit a high pop-up near home plate.

IT'S A

36

"I've got it!" Matt shouted. He took a few steps and looked into the sky.

"No, I've got it!" Lucy was running in from first base at top speed. I stared. What did she think she was doing?

Matt took another step. "I said, I've got it!"

"It's mine!" Lucy didn't stop. She ran right into Matt, knocking him down into the dirt. At the last moment she reached for the ball. But she missed. The ball hit the ground and rolled slowly toward second.

"Ow!" Matt looked as if he was about to cry. "I called for the ball, Lucy!"

"Well, so did I." Lucy bent and touched her knee. "I think you broke my leg!"

Matt groaned. "I think you kicked me in the stomach. On purpose!"

"I did not!" Lucy's eyes flashed.

"I wish I really had broken your leg!" Matt said.

"Will somebody please get the ball?" Mom shouted. Startled, I turned around. The batter was almost to third base. Matt and Lucy were so busy arguing, they had forgotten him.

I rushed over and picked up the ball.

"Home! Home! Throw it home!" I heard Mom yelling. I pulled back my arm and let it fly. It looked as if the ball would get there before the runner. "Catch it, Matt!" I shouted.

Matt was just getting to his feet. He reached out for the ball. So did Lucy. The ball landed in Lucy's mitt. But Lucy's mitt landed in Matt's mitt. And when they turned to tag the runner, they bumped heads and fell down again. The runner was safe.

HOME RUN !

It was the shortest home run I had ever seen!

Not even Brenda felt like eating ice cream after the game was over. "It was all Matt's fault," Josh said. He threw his mitt at the bench as hard as he could. "I'm making a rule. Only the people I like can pet my dog." He glared at Matt. "Not *you*."

"Who cares about your stupid dog?" Matt said. I sat next to him and held his hand. "Anyway, it was Lucy's fault. My stomach still hurts."

"Lucy's always bouncing around," Adam said. "Don't you think that's dumb? She looks just like Dopey when she does that."

"No, I don't!" Lucy tried hard to stand very, very still.

"I don't like you anymore, Lucy," Matt said. "You're always bugging me. You knock me down, and you make faces at me, and you call me lots of mean names—"

"Well, how about you?" Lucy yelled. "You stepped on my hand when we were playing leapfrog, and it really hurt! And sometimes you pick on me, and you ran into me yesterday, and you . . . um . . ." She thought hard. "I don't want to be your friend!"

"Oh yeah?" Matt made a fist. "Well, this is what I think of you!" Quickly he grabbed his stick and finished the sentence he'd started to write before.

"Lucy is an idiot," he wrote.

And now it was Lucy's turn to look as though she might cry.

I thought Lucy and Matt would get over their fight quickly. They always had before.

But I was wrong.

On Thursday afternoon, Matt and Lucy didn't come to practice together, the way they usually did. They didn't play leapfrog together. They didn't grin and laugh. They barely even looked at each other. Lucy hung around with Josh and Julie. Matt stuck with Adam and me.

"Mrs. Antler?" Lucy said after practice started. "I have a new rule."

"What's your rule, Lucy?" Mom asked.

"Everybody whose name rhymes with *cat*

should go and play for the Cardinals," Lucy told her.

"Oh yeah?" Matt stepped forward. "Well, you know what I think? I think we should fire Lucy. The rest of us can play just as well by ourselves."

"Ha!" Julie snorted. "You'd lose every game."

"We already lose every game," Mitchell said softly.

"That's enough." Mom put up her hand. There was a gleam in her eyes. "I have a plan for practice today. First I'm going to divide you into two teams."

"I won't play on Lucy's team," Matt announced.

"Me neither," I added.

"You can make your own teams," Mom told us. "Divide up any way you like."

We gasped. "Really?" I asked with delight. I grabbed Matt's hand. We divided just the way I thought we would—Matt's friends on one team, Lucy's friends on the other.

Mom handed Matt six blue squares made out of cloth. "Everybody on your side gets one," she told him. "You guys are the blue team."

I thought the squares looked like our napkins from home, but I didn't say anything. Matt pinned a blue square on each of us.

"And you guys are the red team," Mom said. She handed red napkins to Lucy, who started pinning them on.

"Slaughter teams!" Adam said. "We're going to rule!"

"We're not keeping score," Mom told him.

"Well, if we were keeping score, we'd win," Adam said.

"Lucy's Rangers rule!" Julie said, putting her arm around Lucy.

Mom told us where to stand around the field. I was between Julie and Josh. Yuck! Both of them had red squares. When I looked around, I saw that Mom had made a pattern: red, blue, red, blue . . .

"I don't want to be next to Brenda," Alex complained.

"How do you play the game, Mrs. Antler?" Danny wanted to know.

Mom stood in the middle of the field. "While one of you is at bat, the others are on the field. You all get a turn to bat," she said.

"If you catch the ball, you can't run with it. You have to throw it. That's the first rule."

"Okay," Danny said. "What's the second rule?"

Mom smiled. "You can't throw it to anybody on your team."

"Booooo!" Josh turned his thumbs down. "That's a dumb rule, Mrs. Antler."

"That stinks," Adam agreed. "I don't want to throw it to Josh. Or Lucy."

Mom frowned. "You don't like that rule?"

"No way!" Matt pretended to faint. Lucy shook her head so hard, I thought it might come off. But they still didn't look at each other.

"Okay." Suddenly Mom got a goofy grin on her face. "I know! I'm not on either team, so everybody can throw it to me!"

"I guess so," I agreed slowly. "But Mom, you're not very good at baseball."

"Throw it to Lucy, then," Mom suggested.

I shuddered. "No, thanks," I told her. "I'll throw it to you."

The first batter was Yin. She hit it right to

me. I thought about throwing it to Lucy at first base, but instead I threw it to Mom. Mom dropped the ball. "Oh, how clumsy of me!" she said. She picked it up and threw it to Lucy. I mean, *over* Lucy. Yin ran to second base and then headed for third.

"Mrs. Antler, catch!" Adam shouted. He threw the ball to her instead of to Alex, who was playing third base. Mom dropped it twice. Then she threw it past Matt, the catcher. Yin slid home in a cloud of dust. "Safe!" Mom shouted. "Home run!"

"Mrs. Antler!" Matt groaned. So did Adam, Julie, and Lucy. Mom put a silly smile on her face. "Sorry, team," she told us. "I haven't had much practice."

One after another, we went up and hit the ball. Then we ran to first. And to second, third, and home. Everybody scored on just one hit. All the fielders were throwing the ball to Mom. And Mom never caught a single throw.

It was fun when you were running, but it wasn't much fun in the field. Once Mom threw the ball to Matt when the runner wasn't anywhere near him. "Sorry," Mom said. She was grinning again. "I just got mixed up."

"Well, you should pay attention," Matt told her.

A few minutes later, Danny threw the ball right to Mom. She dropped it anyway. "Your mom can't be *that* bad," Danny told me. "It's just like the Black Sox."

"The what?" I asked.

"A long time ago, some players on the Chicago White Sox lost the World Series on purpose," Danny explained. "They called those guys the Black Sox after that. It almost looks like your mom is trying to mess up, just the way they did."

We watched Mom throw the ball ten feet over Lucy's head.

"It does look that way," I agreed. "But why would she want to mess up?"

Danny shrugged. "Who knows?"

Brenda came up to bat. She hit a hard grounder to Danny. Danny picked up the ball and started to throw it to Mom. Then he seemed to change his mind. Instead, he threw it to Julie, who was playing first base now. Julie looked surprised, but she caught the ball and stepped on the base.

"You're out!" Mom cried. She winked at Danny and Julie. "Look at that!" she said. "You guys got an out without me!"

After practice that day, when Mom and I were riding home, I told her, "You know, Mom, you weren't a lot of help today."

Mom raised her eyebrows. "Really?" she asked.

I nodded. "We only got outs when we didn't throw the ball to you."

"Hmm," she said. "Well, what do you know!"

I can always tell when Mom is up to something. I frowned at her. "What's going on, Mom?" I asked.

Mom grinned. "Going on? What do you mean?"

But I thought about it all the way home.

Chapter 7

"Lucy will play first base today," Mom told us on Friday. We were about to play the Cubs again.

"We're going to lose for sure," Adam moaned.

"Knock it off, Adam," Mom told him. "Julie, you'll be at second, and Yin will play third."

"Who plays fourth?" Matt asked. He was throwing his mitt up in the air and catching it.

"Fourth?" Mom looked confused.

"You know—second base, third base, fourth base," Matt explained.

Josh snickered. "Fourth base?" he said.

"Don't you even know there isn't any fourth base?"

"Yeah," Julie laughed. "Fourth base—get a load of that!"

"I meant catcher," Matt said. His cheeks were turning pink. "I meant catcher. You know I meant catcher!"

"Matt will catch," Mom said firmly. "And I have an important announcement," she went on. "I won't be playing today."

"Oh, good," Danny said. Josh sighed with relief.

"So if you want to win," Mom said, "you need to do it by yourselves. I'll give you one hint. There's a word you'll need."

A word? I thought. Puzzled, I looked at Matt.

"Is it *mitts?*" Brenda guessed. Mom shook her head.

"How about *baseball bats?*" Adam asked.

"That's two words, you dummy," Josh told him.

"You'll figure it out," Mom said. "Ready to play? Go, Rangers!"

"Oh!" Lucy clapped her hand over her mouth. "Mrs. Antler, I know the word!"

"So do I!" Matt seemed just as excited. "Is it—"

Mom grinned. "Why don't you two say it together?"

Matt and Lucy looked at each other suspiciously. At last Matt opened his mouth, and Lucy opened hers. "Is it *Rangers?*" they asked at the same moment.

"Nope," Mom said. "You're close, though."

Lucy smiled a little. So did Matt. I waited for Matt to say "Jinx!" But he didn't.

"Go, Rangers!" Mom yelled again. This time we all shouted it, too.

C'mon, RANGERS!

"Go, *Rangers!*"

We hit the ball hard in the first inning, but we didn't score any runs. Next it was the Cubs' turn. The first Cubs hit the ball to Adam. Adam dropped it. The batter ran to third base.

"Booooo!" shouted Josh. Julie held her nose.

I watched Lucy to see what mean thing she would say. But she didn't say anything at all. Instead, she gave a little hop. Then she kicked the dirt and shouted, "Come on, Rangers! Let's get them out!"

The second batter hit the ball to Julie. It bounced right between her legs. The runner scored, and the batter made it to second.

"Who said you could catch?" Adam yelled. Brenda stuck out her tongue. I was about to join them. Then I remembered how bad it had felt to get clobbered by the Reds. I didn't want that to happen again. So I didn't say anything.

I looked at Matt behind home plate. He wasn't yelling at Lucy, either. He had a stick, and it looked as if he was writing something in the dirt.

I blinked to see it better. "R-A-N-G-E-"
Rangers rule!

"Rangers rule!" Matt shouted, and Lucy joined in. "Rangers rule!"

Matt waved his arm at Lucy. "Come on!" he told her. "Say it!"

Lucy took a deep breath. "Jinx," she said slowly. Then she grinned, just a little bit.

51

The third batter hit the ball to me. I caught it and started to run across to first base. But I stopped. The batter seemed awfully fast. I knew I could never get there before she did.

For a moment I wished Mom were on the field so that I could throw the ball to her. "Throw it, Catherine!" Mom yelled.

Suddenly I knew I didn't have a choice. I threw the ball to Lucy as hard as I could. The throw wasn't perfect, but Lucy caught it anyway. The batter was out!

I grinned over at Lucy. She gave me a thumbs-up sign.

"Rangers rule!" I shouted. Lucy didn't join me. But I couldn't get angry at her.

Getting that batter out had been too much fun!

Chapter 8

"Aren't you ever going to tell us the important word?" Mitchell asked Mom. It was the last inning of the game, and we were tied with the Cubs, 8–8.

Mom smiled at him. "I still think you'll figure it out."

"Is it *hit?*" Brenda asked. "Or *catch?*"

Mom shook her head.

I tried to think of the things Mom liked to say. "Keep your eye on the ball" was too many words. So was "Good play!"

What else could the word be?

Lucy was batting. "Come on, Lucy!" Mom shouted. She stood up and clapped her hands. "Hit a home run!"

"Come on, Lucy!" Julie stood up, too. So did Josh and Yin. Next to me, I could see Danny begin to get up. And after a moment, so did I.

"Come on, Lucy!" Josh shouted.

I said it quietly, but I said it, all right. "Come on, Lucy!"

Lucy didn't look at us. She took a couple of practice swings. Then she stepped to the plate and swung as hard as she could. *Whack!* The ball sailed way into the outfield. "Fair ball!" the umpire screamed.

"Run, Lucy!" Julie yelled. I watched as Lucy raced to first base. The ball bounced in front of the outfielder. Lucy headed for second base. Someone yelled, "Go, Lucy!" For a moment I didn't know whose voice it was. Then I figured it out.

It was mine!

Lucy touched second base and started

running for third. The outfielder threw the ball. Lucy slid. "Safe!" the umpire called.

Safe! "All right," I shouted. I reached up and slapped five with the person next to me. It was Josh. I could see Brenda hugging Yin.

"A triple!" Danny cried out. "Way to go, Lucy!"

"*Triple*," Mitchell said suddenly. "Is that the word, Mrs. Antler?"

"Not *triple*," Mom told him. "Who's next?" She looked at the list next to her on the bench. "Matt!"

"Oh, it's my turn now?" Matt asked. He picked up his bat and walked to the plate. There was a goofy grin on his face. "I didn't know that."

"Go, Matt!" I shouted. I crossed my fingers, hoping he would get a hit. Even if that meant Lucy would score!

Matt took a big swing—and missed.

"Oh, Matt!" I was disappointed. Still, he had two more chances. I clapped my hands. "Hit it to Timbuktu!"

"Keep your eye on the ball!" Mom ordered.

Matt stuck out his lip and swung a second

time. He swung so hard he knocked himself over. But he missed again. I groaned.

"Come on, Matt!" Danny shouted. "We want to win!"

Suddenly I saw Matt's goofy grin again. "Matt!" I shouted angrily. It looked as if he was trying to strike out on purpose! Like the Black Sox that Danny had told me about. Just so Lucy couldn't score!

"Matt!" I yelled as loudly as I could. "Get a hit!"

Matt didn't look at me. He stepped back up to the plate.

"Matt!" Lucy yelled. I wondered if she had seen that smile, too. "Matt! Drive me home!" She paused. "I mean—drive me to fourth base!"

Matt grinned. And this time it was a real grin. "Okay!" he yelled. "Touch fourth base!" And he slammed the ball past the shortstop.

"Yay!" we screamed when we saw the ball land. Matt was safe at first. Lucy came home—I mean, to fourth base. And now we were winning, 9–8.

"*Nine!*" Brenda said when our turn at bat

was over. "That's the word, Mrs. Antler. Isn't it?"

"No, honey," Mom told her. She clapped as we went to our positions. "Let's go, Rangers!"

The Cubs came up. We couldn't let them score even one run! "Hold 'em, Rangers!" I shouted, and after a moment I could hear Matt and Lucy yelling it, too.

"Hold 'em, Rangers!"

Adam caught a ball, and Josh patted him on the back. Then Julie caught a ball, too. We all cheered. Even me.

When the last Cubs batter came up, there were two runners on base. If he got a hit, we might lose. But he was the same kid who had ended the game the last time we played the Cubs. All we had to do was get him out. Then we would win!

I pounded my mitt and crossed my fingers again. I wanted to yell, but I couldn't think of anything to say. Anyway, my mouth was too dry.

The batter swung. This time he hit the ball right away. It sailed up into the sky. I could tell it would come down right between Lucy

and Matt. "Catch it," I yelled. "Catch it, someone! Catch it!"

Lucy ran in. Matt ran out. "I've got it!" Lucy screamed.

"No, I've got it!" Matt said.

I watched them run toward each other. I could hardly believe it. They're going to crash again, I thought, and we'll lose. The runners were dashing around the bases—

"Teamwork!" I screamed. *"Catch it!"*

At the last moment Matt stepped aside. Lucy reached out. The ball bounced off her mitt. I saw it head for the ground, spinning. Oh, no, I said to myself.

But Matt was waiting. He dropped to his knees and his mitt shot out. The ball fell in, and Matt held on for dear life. "You're out!" the umpire called. "Game's over! Rangers win!"

I let out a yell. Julie jumped on my back. Josh caught me in a bear hug. "Hurray!" we shouted.

Lucy and Matt jumped up and down together next to home plate. "We did it, we did it, we did it!" they were yelling.

Mom came off the bench and patted them

on their backs. "Friends again?" she asked Matt and Lucy as the whole team gathered around.

"Uh-huh," Matt told her. He was still holding the ball. "I don't even remember what we were arguing about."

"We never really stopped being friends, Mrs. Antler," Lucy said, grinning.

"Yeah," Matt said. "We fight a lot—" He looked at Lucy.

"But mostly we get over it," Lucy finished for him.

Mom smiled. "I'm really glad, you two," she answered. "Did you figure out the word that helped you to win today?"

Matt grinned at Lucy. Lucy grinned back at Matt.

"*Teamwork!*" they shouted together. Then they grabbed each other's hands.

"Jinx!" they said. And we all began to laugh.

THE LEFTOVERS #3:

USE THEIR HEADS!

by Tristan Howard

GOOOOAL!
Baseball season is over, and the Rangers are
now a soccer team. Will they be any better at
soccer than they were at baseball?
Only if they remember to use their heads,
not their hands!

COMING IN AUGUST 1996!

L01195